Fun For Hunkydory

by May Justus

Pictures by Sue d'Avignon

GOLDEN PRESS 🦅 NEW YORK

Hunkydory was feeling sorry for himself. Toby, his master, had gone to town, and the puppy was all alone.

"Taking care of the yard is no fun," said Hunkydory. "I'll go out and find some *real* fun."

He scrambled under the gate, and ran into the road.

Slinker, the cat, came out of the barn.

"I've been hunting mice today. It was great fun," he said. "But what are you doing out here? You were left behind to look after the yard."

Hunkydory tossed his head.

"That's no fun," he said. "No fun at all."

And off he went.

Hunkydory came to the pasture field. Andy and Dandy, the colts, were having a race.

"Good morning," called Hunkydory. "That looks like fun. May I come in and race with you?"

"Yes, yes," answered the two colts.

But try as he would, Hunkydory couldn't catch up
with them. Soon his little legs grew tired, and he
began to pant.

"Let's stop awhile, and have some *real* fun," he
called to Andy and Dandy.

"This is fun for us," they said, and away they ran.

Hunkydory set off down the road. Soon he saw Peter Pig rolling and splashing in a mud puddle.

"That looks like fun," said Hunkydory.

"Oh, yes," said Peter Pig. "There's nothing nicer than a mud bath on a hot day. Try it yourself!"

Hunkydory jumped into the puddle. He rolled and splashed about, just like Peter Pig.

Hunkydory got sticky and dirty.

"I don't think it's fun," he said.

"This is fun enough for me," said Peter Pig.

Hunkydory set off once again, sticky and dirty. Soon he saw Old Uncle Billy Goat. He was eating green corn in a field by the road.

"Is that fun?" Hunkydory asked.

"Ma-a-a-a. You bet it is," said Old Uncle Billy Goat. "Come in and help yourself."

But Hunkydory didn't like the taste of the green corn, and soon he felt sick. So he set off once more—sticky, dirty, and feeling sick.

Suddenly, *ker-thud,* a great big hickory nut hit him on the head.

"Please find my nut for me," said Scamper Squirrel. "Then you may come to a nut dinner. Wouldn't that be fun?"

The nut was harder than Uncle Billy Goat's green corn. It made Hunkydory's baby teeth hurt.

"I don't think nuts agree with me," said Hunkydory. "Fun is what I want to find, so I'd better hurry on."

Soon Hunkydory came to a stream. There he saw a
raccoon busily catching fish for his supper.

"May I catch fish with you?" called Hunkydory.
"Fishing looks like fun."

"It *is* fun. Come and join me," said the raccoon.

But Hunkydory wasn't very good at catching fish.
He slipped on the muddy banks of the stream and—
SPLASH! he fell into the cold water.

Poor Hunkydory! Now he was *very* wet.

Hunkydory shook himself and set off down the road again. He came to a house that looked just like his own. On the porch sat a puppy, about the size of Hunkydory.

"He would make a fine playmate," Hunkydory thought. "I know we could find some extra-special fun together."

"Good morning, Friend!" he barked.
"Good morning!" barked the other puppy.
"I'm out hunting for fun," said Hunkydory.
"Will you come along?"

"Oh, I can't," said the puppy. "I'm taking care of the house while my master is away. He always trusts me to do this when he is gone."

Hunkydory turned around and started for home.
He was muddy and tired and sad.

He crept into the yard. Suddenly he saw a chicken
slipping under the fence.

"Bow wow wow! Out you go!" said Hunkydory.

He chased the chicken away. He felt very pleased
with himself.

On the porch he found a bowl of food that Toby
had left for him. Oh, how good it tasted!

"This is much better than corn or hickory nuts,"
thought Hunkydory.

Then he went out to bury a bone. The puppy dug
and dug with his strong paws. My, that was fun!

Suddenly Hunkydory heard a shout. "Hi, Hunky-dory. See what I've brought you!"

It was Toby! Toby tossed him a beautiful, bright red ball.

Hunkydory caught it in mid-air, and brought it to Toby.

"Good dog!" said Toby, and he tossed the ball again.

"Bow wow wow," barked Hunkydory.

"This is fun," he thought happily. "It's better than colt's fun or pig's fun; it's better than goat's fun or squirrel's fun, and much better than raccoon's fun. This is staying-at-home *doggy* fun!"